THE DAY OF THE
DINOSAUR

A special kind of beast
lived very long ago.
Its different forms and names
are very good to know.

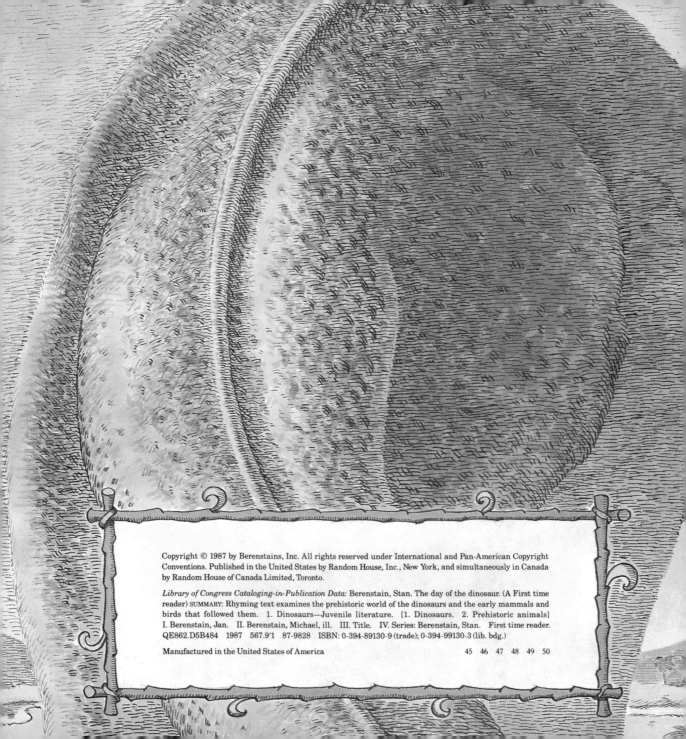

Library of Congress Cataloging-in-Publication Data: Berenstain, Stan. The day of the dinosaur. (A First time reader) SUMMARY: Rhyming text examines the prehistoric world of the dinosaurs and the early mammals and birds that followed them. 1. Dinosaurs—Juvenile literature. [1. Dinosaurs. 2. Prehistoric animals] I. Berenstain, Jan. II. Berenstain, Michael, ill. III. Title. IV. Series: Berenstain, Stan. First time reader. QE862.D5B484 1987 567.9'1 87-9828 ISBN: 0-394-89130-9 (trade); 0-394-99130-3 (lib. bdg.)

Manufactured in the United States of America   45 46 47 48 49 50

THE DAY OF THE DINOSAUR

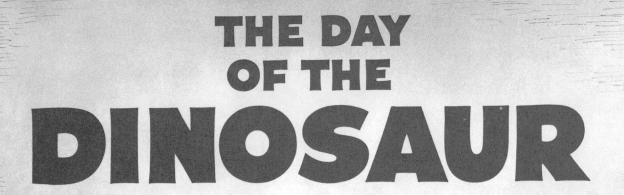

By Stan & Jan Berenstain
Illustrated by
Michael Berenstain

Random House  New York

Long ago,
long, long ago,
before many things
we now know—

before cities,
towns, and roads,

before people,

before birds,
frogs, and toads—

long, long, LONG before—

it was the day of the dinosaur!

Some were small
(as big as your cat).

Fab-ro-SAUR-us

Some were thin,

Mes-o-SAUR-us

others fat.

ER-yops

Some were big...

…very,

very,

VERY

big!

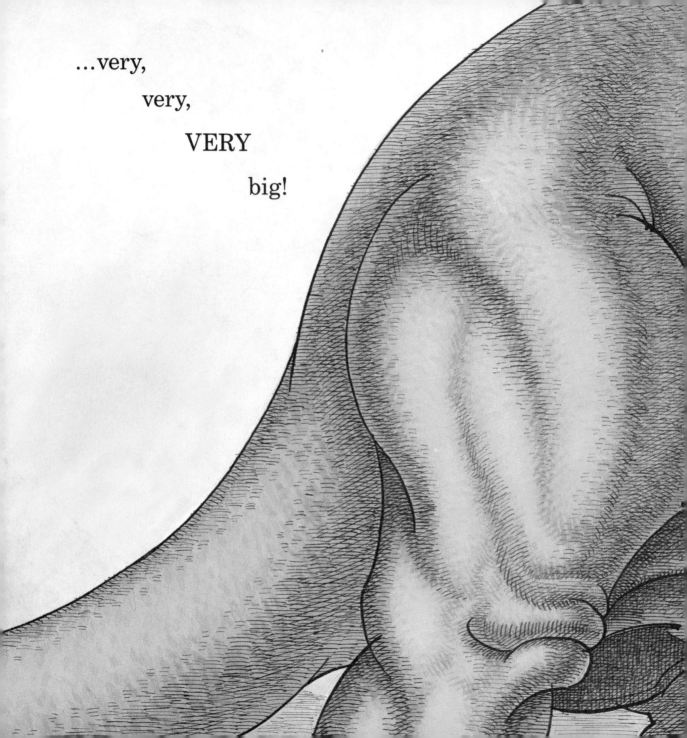

The giant Brontosaurus
was seventy feet tall.
Its name means "thunder lizard."
It was the biggest one of all.

Bront-o-SAUR-us

Dinosaurs roamed
all the earth—
places far and near.
But now that they are gone,
how do we know
they were here?

We know it from
the skeletons
they have left behind,
buried in the earth
for scientists to find.

The bones,
which we call fossils,
tell us much
about the dinosaur.
They tell its size and shape.
They tell us much,
much more.

They tell us
Tyrannosaurus rex
was huge
and fierce
and strong—

Tyr-an-no-SAUR-us rex

with terrible
quick jaws
and teeth
six inches long.

Its ferocity
was famous.
It has long
been told of.

What did
Tyrannosaurus eat?

Whatever it got hold of!

But sometimes Tyrannosaurus
bit off more
than it could chew.
The armored Stegosaurus
was pretty mighty too.

Steg-o-SAUR-us

Its back was armor-plated.
Its tail was tipped with spikes.
(It's very reckless
not to duck
when Stegosaurus strikes!)

Brachiosaurus's nostrils
were atop its head.
They let it breathe while sleeping
in its water bed.

Brach-i-o-SAUR-us

Dimetrodon was a carnivore,
which means its food was meat.
Its great and splendid back-sail
was used to take in heat.

Di-MET-ro-don

The creature Pteranodon
had a twenty-foot wingspan.
It was the biggest flyer ever
since the earth began.

It had a four-foot bill
and a very lofty crest.
When it comes to flying reptiles,
it was the biggest and the best.

(P)ter-AN-o-don

Archaeopteryx
is not an easy word.
But neither was it easy
being earth's first bird.

Ar-chae-OP-ter-yx

After dinosaurs
came other kinds of creatures.
They also had amazing
body parts and features.

The saber-toothed tiger,
of course, had saber teeth.

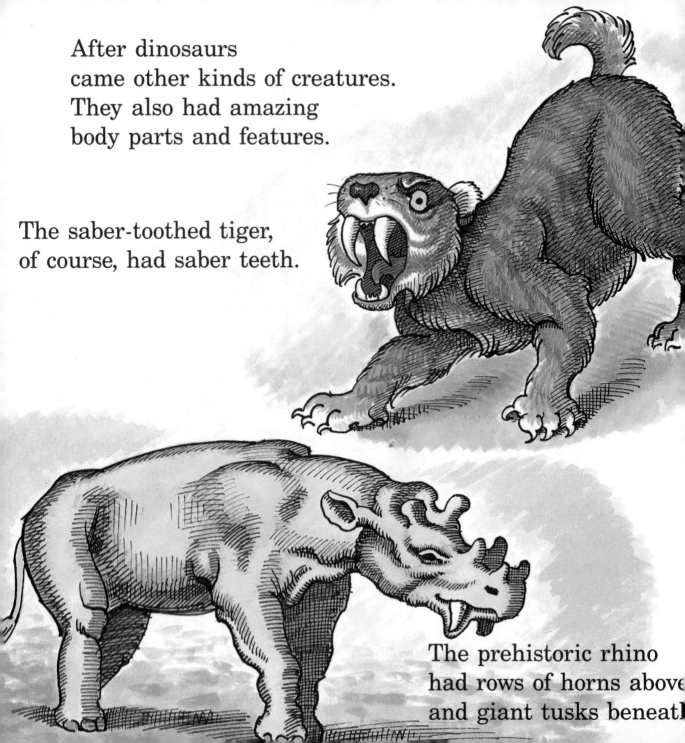

The prehistoric rhino
had rows of horns above
and giant tusks beneath

The moa was a flightless bird.
It stood thirteen feet tall.
It had gigantic drumsticks,
but its brain was very small.

The flightless moa
is now extinct.
(In other words—
there are no moa!)

But it no longer is
the day of the dinosaur.
Except as fossil bones,
they exist no more.

They are now extinct.
Sometimes we wonder why.
Were there just too many
for the food supply?
Was there a great disaster?
Or did it get too dry?

It's the sort
of question scientists
like to think about.
Maybe you'll be a scientist.
Maybe you'll be the one
to figure it out!